*For Katie, Conor,
Jake, Jack, Porfi,
Theo, and Calvin*

IMPRINT
A part of Macmillan Publishing Group, LLC
120 Broadway, New York, NY 10271

ABOUT THIS BOOK
The art in this book was created with pen and ink linework and
digitally colored in Corel Painter and Adobe Photoshop.
The text was set in Sentinel. The book was edited by John Morgan and designed by Carolyn Bull.
The production was supervised by Jie Yang, and the production editor was Ilana Worrell.

Library of Congress Cataloging-in-Publication Data is available.
ISBN 978-1-250-75871-2

Our books may be purchased in bulk for promotional, educational, or business use. Please contact your local
bookseller or the Macmillan Corporate and Premium Sales Department at (800) 221-7945 ext. 5442
or by email at MacmillanSpecialMarkets@macmillan.com.

Imprint logo designed by Amanda Spielman

First edition, 2021

1 3 5 7 9 10 8 6 4 2

mackids.com

There once was a book
a greedy guy took.
That wasn't too clever;
he felt bad forever,
and everyone called him a crook!

A **Tree** for **Mr. Fish**

Peter Stein

{Imprint}
MAKE YOUR MARK
NEW YORK

One morning, two friends met in a tree.

"Hello, Bird," said Cat.

"Hello, Cat," said Bird.

GOODBYE, BIRD AND CAT.

"This is my tree," said Mr. Fish. "It is not for cats or birds."

"But I have climbed high to be in this tree," said Cat.

"And I have flown far to be in this tree," said Bird.

"Climbing and flying are easy," said Mr. Fish.
"I have crawled, rolled, slithered,
and wiggle-waggled to be in this tree."

"But fish don't belong in trees," said Bird.

"They really don't," said Cat.
"A fish in a tree is very weird."

"I will tell you a story," said Mr. Fish.

"Long ago, it rained
for a whole year.

"The lake rose higher and higher
until the water was above
this very tree.

"I lived here," Mr. Fish continued.
"It was my home. And I loved it more
than ice cream on pancakes.

"Nice story," said Bird. "But this tree is not underwater."

"It stopped raining!" exclaimed Mr. Fish. "The water went down! And anyone who is NOT A FISH should leave!"

"Wait a minute," said Cat.
"Fish can't live out of water. They can't breathe."

"That's true," said Bird. "How are you even alive right now?"

They are right! thought Mr. Fish.
No wonder I'm always so uncomfortable.

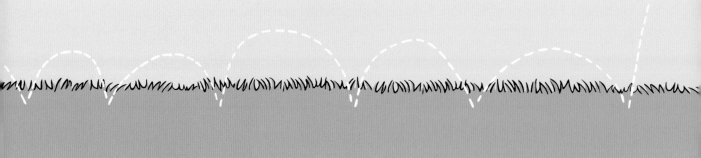

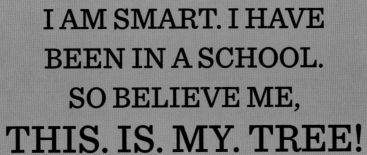

"I will leave because you are too loud," said Bird.
"I have very sensitive ears."

"And I will leave because you are being rude," said Cat,
"which is worse than having fleas."

After a long time went by,
Mr. Fish discovered something.

But then he had a big idea.

Mr. Fish invited all his friends.

It was the worst party ever.

So everyone left.

PARTY POOPERS!

"Who cares about them?" said Mr. Fish to nobody.
"It's MY tree anyway."

But it turned out
Mr. Fish cared.

A lot.

Suddenly he felt lonely.
Very lonely.

His scales sagged.

His gills gagged.

And then . . . waaaaaaaaaaaaa!!

"You are still yelling," said Bird. "Maybe you forgot how sensitive my ears are."

"Maybe," said Cat, "you have forgotten how to be nice."

"I am sorry about your ears,
and I am sorry I was rude," said Mr. Fish.

"I would like to make things better. Will you help me?"

"I will help because you said you are sorry," said Bird.
"I am a very forgiving bird."

"And I will help because you said please," said Cat.
"I'm unusually nice for a cat."

So Mr. Fish shared his plan with Bird and Cat . . .

And when they were done . . .

Mr. Fish shared the tree with Bird and Cat!

fin